THE COLLEGE ADVENTURE

THE WEB IN WHICH WE WEAVE.

 **FriesenPress**

Suite 300 - 990 Fort St
Victoria, BC, Canada, V8V 3K2
www.friesenpress.com

Copyright © 2014 by Lorne W.P. Vanderwoude
Co-author: Leslie Liddle
Illustrator: Barry Mackowosky
First Edition — 2014

ISBN
978-1-4602-5019-8 (Hardcover)
978-1-4602-5020-4 (Paperback)
978-1-4602-5021-1 (eBook)

1. Fiction, Romance, Contemporary

Distributed to the trade by The Ingram Book Company

CONTENTS

DEDICATIONS

First of all, I would like to dedicate this book to my birth mother, Pam Mino, who gave birth to me in a very difficult situation. She loved me so much that she was forced to give me up to a set of parents who could look after me in a way that she was not able to. Secondly, to my wife, Gwen Vanderwoude, who has stood by my side no matter what road I chose to go down. It is due to her love and devotion that has helped me to become the person that I am today. Finally, to my second author, Leslie Liddle, who was also an editor of the first book and has helped me to create my second novel. Without her encouragement, I could not have finished writing these two stories.

—Lorne W.P. Vanderwoude

I would like to dedicate this book to my brother Bob who has passed away, my great family and to my friend, Lori Thompson.

—Leslie Liddle

CHAPTER ONE

"IF I TELL YOU, PLEASE PROMISE THAT YOU WILL NOT TELL ANYONE."

Steve walked into the Jackson Security office just like he did every shift which he worked. He sat down at the main desk and looked at the schedule. His partner, Janet, had been late ever since she had broken up with her newest boyfriend, David. She seemed to be very distracted.

Suddenly, Janet entered the room. Steve noticed that her hair was tied in a ponytail and her eyes were swollen as if she had been crying. "I'm sorry I'm fifteen minutes late," she said slowly, as she hung up her coat.

"You have been twenty minutes late ever since you broke up with David!"

1

"I don't want to talk about it."

One thing about the Jackson twins was that they were known to be very moody. Steve knew better than to push the issue. As a result, the two of them walked in silence as they started their first round.

As they passed the president's office, Steve could not help himself but to ask her a question: "Are you going to check out the president's office?"

"Shut up!" she exclaimed.

Her response was not too surprising, since it was a known fact this was where David and her used to make out. Steve had already assumed that this carried too many memories for her. He knew that losing a boyfriend could be just as painful as losing a job.

The University's cafeteria was a simple room, which had ten tables scattered around. To the back of the room was a huge industrial kitchen, which was where the meals were prepared. There was a room to the side that looked as if it could hold five hundred people. This was the overflow for the dinning room and it was not until they entered the room that she started to be more open with him.

"I'm so sorry, Steve. You don't deserve to be treated like that. It isn't your fault that my life has hit a blank wall."

"I'm so sorry that you had to go through that. David is a real jerk."

"I was the one who broke up with him."

"Why?"

"I was scared. He was talking about marriage and having kids. I'm too young to settle down!"

"Isn't that natural to talk about kids with someone who one might marry?"

"I'm not ready for kids. I'm not ready to settle down. I'm still young. My mother was sixteen years old when she got married and I will not make that mistake!" she shouted.

"You do not have to shout."

"I'm so sorry," she said.

Janet slowly got up and took both coffee cups back to the sink and then washed them. Her long black hair and her slender body always made every guy in Springsville look twice as she walked by. In fact, her sister Shannon, who was built the same way, had the same effect on people as well.

"So, how did you break it off?"

"If I tell you, please promise that you won't tell anyone."

"Okay. I swear that I won't tell."

"That's not good enough. Swear by your grandmother's grave that you won't tell!"

Steve nodded his agreement and then swore on his grandmother's grave. Janet sat down and handed him another cup of coffee.

"As you know, I met David on the University's football field. I first noticed him around six months before. He seemed to be stalking me from a distance, which was creeping me out at first. One morning when I was walking home, I stopped to talk to my sister, who was smoking a cigarette outside the back door of the nursing home. I wanted to ask her if she knew who he was.

"My sister told me that she knew who he was because she works with him. I told her that I did not remember hearing about him before. I asked her what sort of person he was. She asked me if I remembered Mrs. Wilson. I told her that I remembered her as our babysitter, who used to look after us when we were little. My sister informed me that David was her son.

"I remember that I also had a crush on him while we were in grade one. He was the boy who my sister and I switched back and forth with over the years. That is one of the benefits of being twins. In fact, the days when we used to play in the sandbox, it was Shannon who used to play with him as I spent most of my time in the washroom. So you see, contrary to what others believe to be the case, David spent most of his time with Shannon and not me . . . he really should have known better.

"So from that point on, it was no longer creeping me out. It was one evening when I was leaving first year to go to the Library, when I saw him walking as if he was looking for someone. He seemed to be looking all around him, so I stepped right in front of his path and then asked him if he was looking for someone.

"He seemed to be very shocked and tongue tied. I didn't know what else to say so I invited him to take a stroll with me some time, thinking that maybe he could join me on the first round at work."

Janet adjusted her comb in her hair. Her face was a little red with embarrassment. Janet did not blush very easy. Shannon blushed a lot faster than her sister. Steve finished his cup of coffee and then put his cup down and cleared his throat.

"Is our break over? Maybe we should continue on with the rest of the round?"

His partner appeared more distracted lately. As they walked out of the main building that housed major classrooms including the cafeteria, she seemed preoccupied, as if something was on her mind. He tried to be funny, asking her in a serious tone, "Are you looking for someone?"

"Shut up!" was her very harsh response, as she slammed the door right into his face.

He pushed the door open and then raced to catch up with her, calling out: "Are you having your time of the month?"

Well, that was a huge mistake. He carried on walking as fast as he could behind her, yet he could hear every swear word that was in the dictionary, with a few new ones which were perhaps in German. She walked into the second year main area and slammed the door.

As he was walking through the main doors of that area, he saw her crying in the corner of the room. As he approached her, he heard her clearly through her tears say, "Go away you awful jerk!"

He had been standing for some time when he finally felt her arms around his neck, and before he knew it, they were kissing, passionately. Her lips were full and she held her grip firmly around him as his mind raced back to their high school days, when they used to make out in the closet of her parent's house.

Janet pulled away from him, leaving the room, she entered the main hall of the second year dorm. He followed her, and could hear her voice as she called out: "Boy, do I feel much better. As for my personal life," she said, "it's none of your business!" She looked at him. "I'm wondering if you're feeling cold?"

That was when he discovered that his zipper was down. As he looked up, three girls who were dressed in very, skimpy clothing were walking by, laughing and pointing at him. Janet was walking ahead, laughing as she went and now it was Steve's turn to go red.

They entered the other side of the dorm and Janet opened the door, which led them through the main building and toward her father's office. She opened the door and they both walked inside, Janet taking a book from the shelf before they both sat down on the couch that her father would sit students down to talk to them about their behavior. Janet leaned back and stretched out her arms. She had a smile on her face.

"So, do you want to know what I usually did with David on this couch?"

"You probably made out," he said.

"Where did you hear that from?"

"Nancy Grace told me everything that you guys did when you were dating."

"Oh really? What did you and I do in the lounge of the second year dorm?"

"We kissed and you also opened your shirt, which showed the red bra that you are wearing right now."

"Well, that is all what I did with David, and that was all what he saw. I always want guys to get a taste of what they might get if and when I decide to marry. I guess since he and I have broke up, that's his loss."

"Are you suggesting marriage?"

"Oh, Steven, that was the mistake that David made. You better learn from his mistakes or you will get the same results that he suffered."

Janet walked out of her father's office, eventually slowing down when she entered the staff area. Steve found it difficult to catch up with her as she strolled down the main sidewalk that led to the first year dorm. He saw David walking by with her sister; however, if Janet saw them, she didn't let on. Instead, she walked back into the dorm where their office was located.

Chapter Two

"Have you heard about shotgun weddings?"

When Janet opened her eyes it was morning, so she got out of bed, while memories from the day before came to mind. She felt dirty. She had followed through with the plan, which had seemed like a good idea at the time, however, she had a secret that she was keeping from everyone, a secret that she clearly denied.

She stood in front of the mirror and looked at her very slim body. Her face was pale since she did not have any makeup on. Her body was shapely and curvaceous, and after admiring herself, she then stepped into the shower. She often loved baths. She could sit and soak in the bathtub for hours at a time. However, she was in a hurry to get to work. Lately she had been late, which had been making her partner Steve very angry. He had threatened to report her, so she figured that if she kissed him and did some sort of striptease, he could never tell on her to her father. She would just tell him that he knew her. Only her Bible reading father would know what that meant.

Janet walked out of the suite and passed her sister Shannon. Being twins, they would switch their positions at work; Janet would go to the old folks' home, and Shannon would go to the University. Steve and David were unaware that they did this—the thought never crossing their minds. Boy, little did they know the twins.

Janet reached for a smoke as she walked down the sidewalk towards the University. Her parents had been members of the largest church here in Springsville. She wondered what her father would say if he knew that she smoked pot. As she puffed on her drag, it made her feel calm as she rushed to work. Janet took out a bottle of a depressant drug from her bag – Angel Dust, which came from the same supplier. It was easy to get hold of pot and drugs, which would have to be prescribed by a doctor. The care manager was one of the biggest suppliers of pot and drugs in Springsville, which she bought from from a dealer in Oventon, who just happened to be her cousin. She was late again and Steve would be waiting for her.

Janet rushed into the office and apologized for being late.

Janet was very shocked at herself, being so open about her break up with David. It must have been the Angel Dust that had loosened her up, as she found herself kissing Steve and undoing her shirt, showing him her very expensive bra. She had bought it in Oventon with her aunt last week on a shopping spree. She had spoken to her aunt about what she had done with her ex-boyfriend, which made Janet shake her head, knowing that she had to lay off the Angel

Dust. It was making her do and say things that were against her family's beliefs. As she walked toward the office she saw her ex-boyfriend walking along with her sister. Jealously filtered through her body; she did not want him; however, she did not want her sister to have him either. Janet knew what a flirt he was with the girls, and had heard that he was sleeping with Shannon.

Janet walked through the first year dorm and noticed that Steve was following her from a long way off. He probably noticed her sister; however, she did not seem to care who he looked at.

"All you men are all alike," she muttered.

Steve entered the office and found Janet waiting for him. She had removed her security jacket and her shirt, and was now just wearing her bra. She walked over toward his frozen body and then closed the door behind them. Janet was going to make sure that he would not report her to her dad. And she knew exactly how to do it.

It was over an hour when the two of them finally pulled away from one another: "So, what was this for?" Steve asked.

She smiled at him and then slowly put her shirt and jacket back on.

Janet sat down on the bench which was on the north side of the room and then began her little prepared speech.

"I heard that you wanted to report me for being late."

"Me? Oh you have heard wrong," he stammered.

"It doesn't matter what you explain. This is the deal. You open your huge mouth to my dad about your little concern, and I promise I will tell him all about the sex that you and I have been having together on company time."

Steve looked rather shocked as she was giving her little speech.

"Have you heard about shotgun weddings?" she asked.

"What are you talking about?"

"Oh the wedding is not what you should be afraid of. It is what he uses the shotgun for."

"What does he use the shotgun for?" he stammered looking very white.

"He will shoot that whatever you have in your pants." She pointed down at his zipper on his pants. "Do you understand me?"

"Yes."

In a Jackson-like fashion, she handed him a schedule and then walked out of the room.

Janet walked down the hallway and stepped into one of the janitor's closets. As Steve walked by, she stepped out and pulled him into the closet. She ripped open his security shirt and pulled it off of him.

"Now, since you got to see me with only my bra on, it is only fair that I see your top of your naked body."

They kissed in the closet for over an hour. Janet could feel his strong muscles as she ran her hands over his biceps and then down his torso. David had had a little paunch, which really was a turn off, especially for a slender girl like herself. She did not eat any healthier than anybody else in the town. Her metabolism was a lot higher than a lot of the women who lived in this small town called Springsville.

Her thoughts were interrupted by a huge bang that came from the lobby of the dorm. She quickly handed Steve his shirt and helped him put it on and then checked very carefully to make sure that all of her buttons were done up, so that she looked very respectful. After all, she did have a huge set of boots to fill. The Jackson family was a very highly respected family among all the residents of this town. The mayor had called her father "one of the pillars of the community." If only they knew how low she had sunk. Her life was not what her father thought it was.

When the two of them walked out of the closet, Janet broke the silence: "Now," she said, "this is how chemicals are poured into the bottles."

"Yes," said Steve, "I really do thank you for such a wonderful lesson."

It was when they walked away from the students when she realized that there was lipstick on her partner's collar. They began laughing and pointing at them, which made her face turn red with embarrassment, and she was sure that every person in the room could see her face glow.

As the two of them walked outside of the first-year building, Steve finally broke the silence. "I saw your sister walking with your ex-boyfriend yesterday," he said. "Why do you think that he was walking with Shannon?" Janet could not have been more unprepared for such a question, so she walked on in silence, since she didn't know what to say.

"That is because everybody knows that you two split the sheets," he replied very impatiently.

Janet knew too well that in this little town, there was nothing which got past those gossiping mouths. Many of the town's gossipers were from Springsville's largest Baptist church. With the mayor being on the board, there was nothing that this group of people could not do. Maybe that was why she rebelled against the teachings of the church. Taking drugs illegally or pot smoking was not one of the approved activities of the church. However, spreading gossip was not an acceptable activity as well.

Steve's voice broke through her thoughts. "Look, I see David walking over the football field as usual."

She found herself mumbling that she could not give a hoot. At that time she was lighting up as she usually did when she was stressed. She was puffing away at her smoke as Steve was making his observations of what he saw. Yet she was not paying attention to what he was saying. She was just missing what she had with David. She wondered if he knew that she had started smoking Marijuana and taking Angel Dust pills. The pills had made her act in a way that if her father knew what she had done; he would have been quite disappointed in her. Steve was a great guy but he was not as good as David.

"What is bugging you? You have not been yourself since breaking up with your boyfriend. You seemed a lot happier when you were dating him than you are being with me."

Before she knew it, she turned and asked him if he would like to go out for coffee with her after work.

"Sure, that would be so much fun."

"I would like to get to know you better," she said and giggled.

"I thought we got to know each other pretty good already in that janitor's closet," Steve replied with an amused look on his face.

The rest of the shift seemed to be pretty normal. They did a round once per hour. After four o'clock, the sightings of David seemed to stop. That was because he had gone on home for the night. At six o'clock, the shift was over for another day.

Janet felt pretty good about the shift. She put her jacket back on after she had checked the schedule one more time. She knew that Shannon had gone to the nursing home to work with David and that Pam had left for the big city of Oventon for her job at the hospital. Janet blocked Steve from opening the door of the office, feeling that she had taken him off guard as she pulled him down toward her. He was a foot taller than she was, and held on to his kiss for some time. She could feel a sense of freedom inside her since taking the last of the pills, and when Steve had gone to the washroom, she had taken the opportunity to sneak off around the corner of the building to smoke her last joint. Feeling high made her feel better. God just didn't matter to her.

CHAPTER THREE

"I REALLY NEED YOU TO CALM DOWN. PLEASE, DOWN WITH YOUR CLAWS."

The walk back to Janet's place was very uneventful. Steve was taken back so much by her behavior that it made him feel sick in his stomach. He watched her as she walked on ahead of him. She was not acting like her sister. His body trembled as she unlocked the door to her small but nicely decorated apartment. As he walked in he saw the place was painted in pink. This color seemed to be almost every girl's favorite color. The apartment looked like the place which his sister had kept before she moved to Oventon. Boy, did he sure miss his big sister, Kelly. He missed his sister and her little girl so much, his heart ached.

His mother told her that as long as she was living in sin, she was no longer invited at their place. It had been years since he had seen the little girl or his older sister. His mother had told him that if she heard that he had ever went to see her, she would ban him from the family house.

Janet seemed to be in a very interesting mood. She set up a movie for the two of them to watch and then went into the kitchen. Steve could hear the sound of pots rattling as he sat on the living room couch and watched the movie. Then out of the blue, the smell of pancakes, bacon and eggs floated throughout the air of the whole apartment. The Jackson girls were all known for their cooking.

Before he knew it, a plate was placed in front of him. They ate the products of her labor in silence, and then afterwards, she put both plates into the dish washer in the kitchen. After that she came into the living room where he had been watching the movie for the past hour. Without warning Before he knew it, he found her lips interlocked with his. Her breath sure smelled like the bubblegum which she had been chewing right after breakfast.

He was not aware of how long the two of them kissed. She had removed his shirt and was rubbing his strong biceps, which really turned her on. Steve could feel her lips as she kissed his chest. The one thing he wanted to do was to deliver a hickey right on her neck. In high school, he had seen other guys do this to their girlfriends, right in the hallway, so, without further hesitation, he did so.

Later after they got off of the couch, he noticed the red mark on her neck. To his surprise, she did not try to cover it up. As he was leaving to go back to his place, she patted the red mark on her neck.

"So, you really do believe that you have done something to brag about?"

He blushed and hung his head. Sucking on her neck had been very sexy; however, the way she spoke of it made him feel dirty."I sure hope father does not ask where I got this from," she said, her voice breaking his thoughts.

She was pointing to the red mark, thus making him feel pretty scared, and then continued with her assault on his intelligence.

"What should I tell my father? Maybe I should explain to him that you and I have been rolling in the wet sheets. I do wonder if he is going to use his gun . . ."

Steve had finally had enough. He raised his voice and cut her right off.

"We have never been sexually active, Janet! How could you ever tell him that bunch of crap?"

"I really need you to calm down. Please, down with your claws. I was just messing with you. I always wanted one of those things during a make out session," she said.

Steve had heard that the Jackson twins could be drama queens. This was the first time that he had seen her wild side. The more she was away from her ex-boyfriend, the wilder she got. Maybe this relationship was not really for him, and somehow, he had to think of a way out of it. Yet, it was not going to be easy; she could easily blackmail him for what mattered the most in his life. His job.

Chapter Four

"Is your ex-boyfriend back on the market?"

She watched him walk down the sidewalk and start on his way home. A sudden guilt rushed upon her as she watched him walk all alone. She really did enjoy the make out sessions which she had been doing with him ever since she had broken up with her sweetheart, David. Boy did she miss him. She missed the fun things that they did together and she sure missed his way of coping with the events of life. Janet would often daydream to keep her sanity about him. She really missed his sense of humor and his ability to make her laugh.

As she thought about her relationship with Steve, her heart began to quiver. The way that her sister Shannon had put it, the plan to get rid of David really seemed to make sense. Now, she was not too sure why she really got rid of the guy? She looked at the picture of her and David and reflected on happier times when they were together. *What had happened to them?* She wondered. *Was it because they had grown a part?* Or was it because of her secret that only she knew?

Janet was starting to feel that the position which she had put Steve in was not very comfortable for him. She was beginning to sense that he wanted out of their so called relationship. However, she also knew that as long as they were going out together, he would not report her for her bad attendance record. As she sat in the living room, watching television, she began to think of what she would do in order to get away from her situation. Janet hated the idea of being in a place for too long.

There was a pamphlet that she had found on the coffee table. It was all about a special "Earn while you learn program" at the Oventon hospital. This was for the LPN program due to the fact that there was a huge short fall of nurses. Her sister, Shannon, was a candy stripper at the same hospital. Janet had also performed the same role when she had changed shifts, and had come along pretending to be her sister. No one had been the wiser.

The schedule at her work was quite easy to fix. She gave herself a week off with the excuse that she wanted to give the new security member more shifts. Penny had just joined the security team at the "Jackson University." She had reddish straight hair, which hung down to her shoulders, a button nose, and very fine features. She really looked very hot to Janet. If she ever swung the other way, this would be a girl she would be interested in. However, God would not agree with that either!

Janet got up around seven the next morning. Shannon was getting ready for her shift at the nursing home. Janet had been separated from David for two weeks, and therefore was a little surprised when Shannon asked her: "Is your ex-boyfriend on the market?"

The question had raised a sore point: "Is he back on the market? You're acting like he is a piece of meat for sale!" she snapped back at her.

"I've noticed that you and Steve can't keep your hands off each other. It isn't fair that you are keeping two men all to yourself!" she shot back.

"You don't have to be so touchy," she replied.

Janet really was not pleased that her sister wanted to have her ex-boyfriend. She always wanted what she had thrown away. What would happen if she just wanted him to be tossed to the side of the road? That would be her right. For him to be left alone for the rest of his life. Yet, deep inside her, she knew that this was not possible. David did not belong to her like owning a car. And boy, did she yearn for a *Smart* car, her only hurdle was to convince her father how great they were and easy on fuel. Maybe her future husband would buy her one?

The two sisters went separate ways. Janet drove off to spend a week with her auntie. Oventon was not that long of a drive and the weather was nice as she drove down the highway.

Familiar sights began to pop up as she entered the city. She could see the famous "Blue Line Taxis" and of course, "Gales Taxi" service. Her uncle had worked for "Blue Line Taxi" for the past twenty years, and as she drove down the empty street at one in the morning, she became aware of a new blue taxi, the driver honked his horn and pulled up alongside her.

It was her uncle and he asked her to meet him in town over at "Ernie's Pancake House."

They sat together in the restaurant eating "all you can eat pancakes" for just $6.99, with all the toppings you can handle. Janet spoke to her uncle, explaining to him why she had just joined the "Earn while you learn" program at the hospital.

"Your wife is a RN at the hospital. She could show me the ropes of being a nurse," she said.

"Why are you moving to Oventon? How did David feel when you told him that you were going to move?" he asked.

"David and I are no longer friends or an item."

"Why? He's a very nice guy."

"He wanted a serious relationship. I am too young to settle down to have ten kids like other girls have done in Springsville."

Just then a pot pipe fell out of her pocket. She was hoping that her uncle would miss the whole situation. However, he was way too fast for her according to her liking.

"Since when did you start to smoke pot?"

"Ever since Stacia introduced it to me six months ago. I smoked a little at first, but slowly I have been buying more and more."

"Does your dad know about your new habit?"

"I have not told either of my parents about this. I have blackmailed Steve; so, if he does tell on my actives, I will report him to dad that he is sleeping with me. Steve is so scared that I will go through with my threat."

"How do you believe that God will feel about your situation?"

"I do not personally care what this so-called God feels about my business! I am so sick and tired of everybody shoving this religion down my throat!"

"You don't have to shout!" he responded very quickly and calmly.

Janet called for the waitress and asked her for a coke and rye. Her uncle looked on as Janet grabbed the glass from the waitress and then chugged the drink down, before slamming the glass on the table. She then went back for a third helping of pancakes, taking a huge serving that even her uncle could not have finished eating. Afterwards, she chugged down another coke and rye, drinking ten glasses within an hour, before excusing herself from the table.

Janet went to the rest room and took five pills of Angel Dust. Boy, when she was high on that drug as well as her father's Prozac, she always felt invincible. Her auntie in Oventon had once told her that Prozac was an antidepressant, which affects the chemicals in the brain that may become unbalanced and cause depression, panic, anxiety or obsessive compulsive symptoms. There was just one time when she felt that all the germs in the room were out to get her. So she cleaned the entire bathroom from top to bottom in her birthday suit. After that she cleaned her body in the shower for over one hour.

Janet found herself to be very light headed and very weak. She felt her uncle carry her out to his taxi, and from there, he drove her to his house. She was way too drunk to be taken to her religious auntie, yet he was unaware just how high she was to be taken to her aunt's place. If he did notice, he didn't let on. He put her seat belt on and she smiled at him as he eventually pulled away from the curb. From that point—everything went black.

CHAPTER FIVE

"SHE STOPPED RIGHT IN HER TRACKS WHEN SHE SAW STEVE STANDING THERE WITH PENNY AT THE DOOR."

Steve shook his head as he looked at the new schedule. He noticed that Janet had taken a whole week off as part of her summer holidays. He sat down in the huge chair that Janet used in order to write out the schedule, when he noticed a new name. Penny.

Steve had heard from the town's gossip that the twin's first cousin was going to cover while Janet was on holiday. According to the latest gossip, Janet was visiting her auntie. Lately, Janet seemed to be a little out of sorts. He sure hoped that she soon would be feeling better.

Just as he was looking at the schedule, he noticed that it was time to do his first round. He quickly logged on to the computer, and signed on to his shift, which was the new way of "clocking in."

Steve walked out of the office and noticed a girl dressed in a security uniform, sitting down on one of the couches that were set in a semi-circle. She was a true red head with green eyes. He was sure that she was Penny but he had to make sure.

"Hello," he said as he walked up to her.

"Well, hello, Steve."

She spoke to him as if she knew who he was. Then he noticed her name tag, which all of the security guards wore. "Penny" was the name on the name tag.

"It's nice to meet you, Penny."

"Do you honestly remember me?"

Steve had to be honest with her. He did not remember who she was. His mind had a gone completely blank and his face must have revealed the lack of memory.

"You and I used to play together in the school's playground. We used to be friends through grade one to grade six, before our family moved to Oventon."

Steve then remembered that she was the Penny who was a cousin to the twins. His face grew very red with embarrassment. She smiled and then laughed at his huge mistake at remembering who she was. He suddenly recalled that he had to do the first round of the night. Steve pointed at the door to inform Penny that they were going to do the first round, so they set off walking through the first year dorm, and then onto the main building where the offices for the staff were situated.

As they walked through the hallways, Steve noticed that she had a very nice figure. Her hair was not black like the twins were. Her hair was very dark, red, and looked darker than it was. They walked past the twin's father's office and she said, "Are you and Janet sleeping together?" which really shocked him. It was a question that he did not expect her to ask.

"No. Why are you asking me such a stupid question?"

"I heard Janet and Shannon talking about making out."

"Janet and I have kissed; however, we never slept together."

She smiled at him and walked on. He could never figure out what people were saying behind his back. As they walked on he couldn't help but ask her some questions which were burning in his soul.

"Do you have a boyfriend?"

"I used to be married. We had an excellent marriage until one day, around five years ago, when I found my husband in bed with my sister. I was pregnant with our second child. I divorced that controlling jerk and I have never spoken with my sister for the past five years. He used to beat me until I was black and blue. So I guess that was a blessing."

He was surprised to discover that she had kids, however, more so, that she was barely over thirty years old. "So," he said, "how old are your kids?"

"I have two daughters: Anne is ten and Rose is six."

They walked on until they arrived at the dinning room of the University. Steve always remembered the coffee times which he had with Janet. He sure missed her so much. He got himself and Penny a cup of coffee.

"Do you take cream or sugar?" he asked very nervously.

"I usually take mine black," said Penny. She giggled as she took off her yellow security jacket.

He noticed that all the Jacksons were very slender and in very good shape. While he sipped his coffee, Penny realized that he was staring at her and told him that if he took a picture of her it would last longer.

"I'm so sorry for staring. That was quite rude of me."

"That's okay," She said. "You men are all alike. You always have one thing on your minds." Then she giggled.

"What are you talking about, Penny?"

"I read once in a medical journal that you guys think of sex every so many times per minute. My ex-husband thought about sex so much that he had a huge collection of porn magazines and videos under his bed. He always thought that I never knew about his collection."

"I'm not like that!" Steve protested. In fact, he was rather insulted that she even suggested that he was like a pervert.

He must have shown his disappointment and disapproval when she looked down at her cup as she spoke."I'm so sorry for my rude comments," she said. "I was out of line then for making such accusations."

"That's okay. You must have gone through a rough part of your life when you were married to your ex-husband."

It was the end of their first coffee break. Steve was relieved that she was not like Janet. If she had been, they would have been in the janitor's closet making out with each other. He certainly hadn't complained. The smell of Janet's perfume and the feeling of her slender body aroused him; however, he was fond of Penny, who was built very similar to her cousins.

The shift was very uneventful. Steve showed her the ropes of how to sign in and out by using the new key pass. The computer would record how many times and when they would pass through certain doors throughout the campus. It was at the end of the shift when he found himself offering to walk her home.

After seeing Penny home he said goodbye, and then noticed a young red-haired girl appear at the front door.

"This is Anne." Penny sheepishly introduced her to him.

The young girl shook his hand and said hello. He was amused at how well mannered she was, not a little brat that he had envisaged when he first saw her. Moments later, another little girl came to the door yelling, "Mommy, Mommy, you're finally home!" The young girl stopped in her tracks when she noticed a strange man standing with her mommy at the door.

"This is my youngest daughter Rose," said Penny, pointing at her to Steve.

As Steve walked home, he had a new appreciation for his new work partner. She was a decent person who was looking after her family by herself the best way she could.

When Steve finally got ready to go to bed, he reflected on his time wth Penny, and their first shift together. His first impression had been that she was some sort of loose and fancy free girl, who liked to sleep around, which made him feel guilty. While he lay in bed thinking about about things, he suddenly wondered how Janet was doing.

CHAPTER SIX

"MY WIFE AND I ARE SEPARATED," HE REPLIED, LOOKING DOWN AT HIS SHOES.

Janet woke up to the sound of an alarm. The noise sure hurt her head as it rang. She looked around at unfamiliar surroundings, and then she remembered—she was at her uncle's place. Flashbacks of the liquor and pot that she had consumed came to mind.

She walked into the kitchen and could see her uncle's new wife making breakfast. The smell and familiar sight of bacon eggs was what her family had every morning. Her new auntie didn't look at her when she entered the room, but Janet guessed that she had eyes in the back of her head, knowing she was there behind her, she said, "I heard that you had quite a wild night, young lady."

"It was nothing too special, auntie. I only had a few drinks with supper last night."

"Well, you better not be telling that to your other auntie. She will be turning you over her knee and be giving you a huge spanking. This is the spanking that you should've had years ago. I tell you, the nerve of you smoking pot and drinking the way that you are, young child. Your father would not be too pleased if he knew that you were acting in that manner."

"Auntie! I am so sick and tired of you religious people preaching at me all the time about my so-called sins. Your gossiping is just as much a sin as my smoking and drinking."

"I do not gossip, I share prayer requests with those ladies of the church who are very concerned for the needs of others," her auntie snapped back.

"I am sure that your over eating is one of the spiritual gifts that God has given you."

Her auntie ignored what she had just said. She put the food down on the table and then told her to eat her breakfast so she could get ready for her interview at the hospital. Then she left the room in a huge huff as she often did when she was angry over her husband's niece's actions.

Janet sat down with some pancakes, while helping herself to eggs and bacon. Boy, could she do with another smoke. Her body was filled with pain from the over drinking into the early hours of the morning. Her uncle walked into the kitchen. He had worked the night shift for the past twenty years. He informed her that the bus was leaving in thirty minutes for the hospital. That was what he always called the taxi car when ever he had to give a family member a ride as a favor. He was always so kind and gentle, and Janet wished that her auntie could be just as nice as he was.

The drive to the hospital was rather uneventful. When they arrived, Janet bid her uncle goodbye, and then made her way into the building. The hospital reminded her of an old army base; the corridors were long and maze like in appearance. She was led to a room and there was a group of people in there, waiting for her.

Her family sat waiting for her: father, mother and her sister Shannon, all sitting there looking at her. Standing beyond the doorway was a young doctor. He cleared his throat as he began to speak: "Janet, my name is Doctor Ratherton, and as you've probably guessed already, this is an intervention. Your family loves you very much." He took a moment to look at them before asking them if they had anything to say.

One by one her family spoke up, all expressing the help she needed to stop her from drinking and smoking pot. What really ticked her off was that one of the members was Stacia herself. She was her supplier of the pot. Her fake words of love were enough to make her want to throw up.

Then the doctor spoke again: "Would you be willing to go on a treatment program here at the hospital," he said, "in order to get you the help you so desperately need?"

Well, what choice did she have? Her family and the community of Springsville were so controlling and snoopy that they had the power to ruin her life, so she had little choice other than to nod in agreement.

It was not the fact that they all wanted to help that bothered her. It was more that this was to be filmed as the newest "Intervention" program that the city's new television station had began to set up in order to boost television ratings for their programs. She was never sure if it was money which motivated her family or love. Either way there was love involved. Her family had such a love for money that it was not funny to which lengths they would go to achieve more and more of it. The Jesus she read about in the Bible did not like money at all. He never had anything good to say about it. In fact, Jesus said that it would be easier for a rich man to go through an eye of a needle than it would be for him to get into heaven.

Her life was far from perfect. She had many weaknesses, and she was sure the dear Lord would hardly approve. One of her weaknesses was good-looking men in white uniforms, doctors, which really turned her on.

The first thing that the hospital did was to assign her a mentor, who was supposed to help her stop using pot. His name was Gary Rothchild. He had Blonde hair and was quite tall, and married with three children.

The process of getting off pot was rather harsh and painful. The withdrawal symptoms were harsher than getting high. Her body was addicted to the drug and needed it to function.

Janet was staying in a special wing of the hospital. She was watching television when there was a knock on the door. She called out for the caller to enter, and when the door opened she could see a doctor standing in the doorway dressed in a red pull-over and black trousers. Janet admired his good figure and great looks. "I was in the area," he said, "and I thought you might like to go out for a cup of coffee?"

"What would your wife think of you hanging out with other women?" she asked in a shocked tone.

"My wife and I are separated," he replied looking down at his shoes.

That settled it for Janet. She asked him to wait for her while she got ready. She dressed herself in a very nice blouse with a pair of black pants, along with some new pumps that she had bought not too long ago. After leaving the hospital grounds, the couple walked off together on the sidewalk.

There was a very nice pizza place around the corner from the hospital, which served the usual meal of pizza and coke. Gary told her many jokes, and also how he had met his wife, who had been one of the candy strippers at the hospital. He had been a nurse's aide before becoming a doctor. She had helped him through med school, and some time after, she became pregnant and they had three wonderful children.

After a short time together he checked his watch and told her that they better be getting back to the hospital. Their time together had been eventful, and they had got to know one another a lot better.

When they returned to the hospital, the doctor walked Janet to her room, but just as he was about to leave, she began to embrace him. The couple began kissing and although Janet knew that it was wrong, she was powerless to stop herself while allowing him to stroke her body. Janet would be furious if this ever got out, or so she thought, so they would have to be careful.

"Thank you for a great time," he said, and then he opened the door and left the room.

Janet stood in a complete state of shock. He was a married man. She cared little if he was separated or not, this was completely wrong. Then she thought back to what she had done to Steve. Having made out with him, she then blackmailed him, which now caused her heart to ache. She really missed him and now wondered if he was okay and what he was doing with his life.

CHAPTER SEVEN

"ALL I HAVE TO DO IS TO REMIND HIM OF HIS DAUGHTER'S EXTRA ACTIVITIES."

The sound of the alarm clock woke Steve from an unsettling dream. His heart was racing. In the dream he had been running away from a car that kept on following him. The car was black—a very dark black, which had unnerved him. Then suddenly the scene changed from outside in the rain on a dark street, to the basement in the inside of an old church. A huge storm had made all the lights go out, making the piano player cry and the poor minister wail with frustration. That was before the sound of the alarm awoke him from his nightmares.

Steve got out of bed and stepped straight into the shower, before getting dressed for the day ahead. He made his way into the kitchen for some breakfast; he opened the fridge and noticed that he was out of milk, eggs and bacon, so decided to go out for breakfast instead.

He walked down the street from his apartment building and could see Penny making her way toward town. She was heading to the same restaurant as Steve, and they happened to meet at the doorway

"So, what are you doing here this morning?" he asked her.

"My mother came down for the week. She's now looking after the kids, however, it means that I have the day off so I can get my shopping done before I have to go to work tonight."

Her dark, reddish hair was held up in a ponytail, the intense color sure making her green eyes stand out. Penny looked just as slender as the twins did. They decided to take a seat at a table in the corner of the restaurant. Steve looked at her, admiring the way her eye liner was done just perfectly, and the way she looked up with those innocent eyes, which always made her look so cute.

They ordered the same for breakfast: eggs, bacon, toast and jam. It was the "special," which the restaurant served every morning. At $3.99 the "special" came with coffee or tea.

They sat in silence as they waited for their orders to arrive at the table. When their breakfast was served Penny asked Steve for the salt. As they started to eat, they noticed that they were being watched by some ladies from a nearby table. They were aware of the local gossip and therefore knew that their being together would inevitably give the town's gossipers more talk about. In such a little town as this, nothing was secret. All they could do was to maintain good conduct in the hope that they would avoid any unnecessary chatter among the locals.

After breakfast, the two of them left the restaurant. As they walked down the street, Steve turned to Penny and asked her if she wanted to see his apartment. Given that she had the whole day to herself before starting the night shift, she nodded her head in agreement.

Steve closed the door to his apartment and then took Penny's jacket and hung it up. Then, they kissed for the first time—a kiss which lasted a long time.

They spent the rest of the afternoon with each other in what was a great experience for both them. While sitting together on the couch, they watched some movies. Steve had never felt so safe being in a girl's arms, and for Penny, the feeling was mutual. Steve had accepted her children, and that in itself made her feel more attracted to him. They embraced one another and kissed passionately until the time arrived for them to get ready for work.

They were on the same shift once again: the 10–6 shift. She kissed him once again, this time placing her tongue in his mouth. French kissing was not a usual thing for him to do; he could taste her mouthwash as he held onto her kiss. Steve caressed her body, running his hands over her thighs and her stomach; even Janet's body was not as slender. He was reminded once again how safe he felt being with her and was enjoying the experience.

The couple held hands as they left the apartment, making their way toward the University to begin the night shift. A feeling of guilt came over him, knowing that in a way, he was cheating on Janet.

He sure hoped that her father wouldn't find out. That wouldn't be so good for his working career, which made him nervous.

The two of them walked through the doors of the first year dorm, acting quite innocently. When they reached the office, Steve closed the door and then went over to the office desk and signed them in on their shift. It was while they were on their first round when Steve hesitated just outside of Janet's father's office. He had heard so much of what Janet and her ex-boyfriend got up to in that office. The graphic details of their activities were enough to make a saint blush.

The two of them walked past the main door of the president's office, and for the first time Steve noticed how huge the room really was. *No wonder Janet always liked to take David to this room,* he thought. The place offered a lot in terms of comfort; coffee and tea was available in one corner of the room, and a cooler with beer, coolers and pop, which was located right behind the desk. This was where her father entertained his guests.

They looked around the room and were amazed at how far the University went to make sure their president was very comfortable. As Penny reached for the door knob, Steve hugged her from behind, embracing her tightly.

"We do have to get going in order for us to finish our first round, cowboy," she said. "We have to swipe all of those sensors which are all on a timer. It is not like it used to be, my dear friend."

"I couldn't control myself, sweetie," he replied, as he slowly released and pulled away from her. He then opened the door for her in order that they could continue on their rounds.

They made the next sensor just in time, and just as he swiped it, he turned and lifted her up onto a table. They were in the science lab which was the next sensor. Steve leaned over and kissed her very deeply on her lips.

"You do realize that if Mr. Jackson ever caught you, both of us could be suspended."

"I am aware," he replied, as he kept kissing her.

"You are not that concerned that this could happen?" she asked.

"All I have to do is to remind him of his daughter's extra activities."

"What?"

"His daughter is hooked on pot and she has been seen making out with one of her fellow workers," he explained.

"So, who has she been making out with lately? I've heard that she's known to be quite loose."

"I am not at liberty to say since it would be spreading gossip."

"Well, that hasn't stopped you before," she said.

Steve knew better than to argue with anybody, especially with a woman. Instead, he just laughed and picked her up, before placing her back on the floor.

"I sure love your muscles. Do you work out every day?"

"I do go to the University gym sometimes when I get the money," he said. "I have to pay around ten dollars per time."

The rest of the round passed by quickly, and in little time they were back in the office. Steve remembered what Janet had told him what she used to say to David when ever she wanted to make out with him.

"I've noticed that there are no security cameras in this room. I do wonder what we should do about this."

Steve turned around to see his partner had taken off her yellow security jacket. Boy, did she look hot in her black security sweater. At that moment she looked even hotter than Janet ever did. She had a cute face and she was slender, yet curvier than the twins. He couldn't control himself and he pulled her into his arms, the two of them French kissing, until they were distracted by a loud bang that came from the lobby of the building

The two of them separated and then headed towards the office's door.

CHAPTER EIGHT

"THE TWO OF THEM KISSED AND THEN SHE WALKED OUT OF HIS OFFICE."

The drug recovery was going quite well for Janet, and after all, she was seeing Gary on a regular basis. After each session, the two of them would go out for a meal or to the bar for drinks. She had been drunk so often that her auntie decided to kick her out of her house until such a time that she got her life back together again. Gary had offered her his guest suite, which was in the basement of his house. Her auntie accepted the arrangement because she had no idea of her relationship with a married man.

One evening Janet was relaxing after one of her evening sessions with the doctor. She was in the guest suite and watching a movie, when there was a knock on the door. When she stood up to answer, she was shocked to find Gary's wife standing at the door. She was in a very nice pink dress and her hair was done up attractively in a bun.

"So, you are my husband's latest project," she blurted out.

"I guess that you can call me that," Janet giggled.

"I really wanted to get to know you," she said, explaining her presence at her door at ten o'clock at night.

"Would you like to come in?" Janet offered.

"I would love to. Thank you," she said and walked in.

The two of them sat down on the couch and began chatting. Gary's wife explained to Janet how her husband had a great heart; however, he had many weaknesses, which she had had to put up with for many years. Having listened, Janet asked her what such a wonderful man could have in terms of any weakness.

"He likes to have more than one sexual partner."

Janet felt as if she was staring through her soul. Then his wife leaned over toward her and whispered into her ear. "The last girl who had a sexual relationship with my husband ended up in the hospital with a broken hip, smashed jaw, and now she's in a wheelchair. I would sure hate to see that pretty face of yours rearranged. So," she said, "here's some advice. Please stay away from my husband, you little slut!"

The woman got up from the couch and then left, leaving Janet sitting alone, trembling. When Janet finally got up she stood looking at her shaking body in the mirror and she had turned noticeably white with fear.

That was quite a huge experience for Janet; she had never had to endure such a violent threat toward her throughout her entire life.

After all, it was Gary who had come onto her and he had insisted that they were separated. Wow! That did not seem to make sense. One of them was lying to her. She was not sure who was telling her the truth. So, she decided to ask Gary what was going on.

Janet phoned a taxi in order to go to his work place, which was at the hospital. She was sure that he had another office elsewhere; however, uncertain as to its location. When she arrived at the hospital she began to shake and sweat; she was scared and nervous of what she would find. Would she find him in the arms of another woman, or worse of all, in the arms of his so-called ex-wife? What would she find? Would he tell her that she had misunderstood what he meant? Even so, how could she have misunderstood the way he held her and kissed her.

When Janet finally arrived at his office, she was relieved to find him sittting doing his paperwork. He asked her to come on in, so she sat on the chair facing the front of his desk.

"Your wife came to see me today," she said. She started very slowly and carefully.

"Is that so?" he replied.

"She offered to rearrange my body if I didn't stop seeing you."

Gary got up out of his chair and walked over to her and hugged her. "So," he said, "you've met the old bat. Please don't be afraid of her. She's crazy but harmless."

Janet looked into his innocent looking eyes. He was an expert in mind games, and maybe if Janet truly understood his attitude toward women, she would have walked straight back out the door.

"I'm so sorry for doubting you," she said.

The two of them kissed and then she walked out of his office. As she walked out of the office building, she really felt that everything was just going to be fine. She was proud that it had been over two weeks since she used pot. Her life seemed to be getting back on track.

The next morning, Janet woke up to the sound of her alarm. She looked over at her alarm clock and discovered that it was five o'clock. It was time for her morning jog. When she went for a jog, she often used the time to think about her life. She thought about her friend, David. How she met him on that football field at the University. Then how he got too close to her and how she got rid of him through a deceiving trick. She had someone take a picture of Shannon and him kissing. The worst part was that it was her and her boyfriend who kissed in that bathroom. She had switiched places wth Shannon once again, just as they had done many times before, leaving Steve and David, none the wiser.

While out jogging she started thinking about where her life was going. She had dropped a guy who had loved her since their early days in the sand box. With the drugs now leaving her system, her head was finally beginning to clear. She thought about David and Steve, and now beginning to doubt whether her relationship with Gary was really worth it.

After her morning jog she returned to her apartment suite. She was beginning to feel sick, and hopeful that she was not coming down with the flu. There was after all, a very bad strain of the flu going around the city. Janet made her way to the bathroom and hung her head over the toilet, and wondered if she should make an appointment to see the doctor, given that she may be in need of some drugs to combat the virus.

It was the next day when she was finally able to see a doctor. After running some tests, Janet waited in the doctor's office for him to return with her results. When he came back, he wore a serious expression. He then told her the results and her face turned white.

Chapter Nine

"Are you trying to kill me?"

Penny and Steve raced out into the lobby area of the dorm. They were just in time to see two girls in a huge cat fight. The larger girl was around three hundred pounds. She was large with short red hair. The other girl had long, blonde hair and was one hundred pounds soaking wet. Before the two of them could stop the larger girl, she had already pinned the skinnier girl up against the wall and slapped her until her nose was bleeding.

Penny and Steve pulled the larger girl away, and while Steve managed to secure her, Penny called for the police and emergency services.

When the police arrived they arrested the large girl, while the other girl was helped into the ambulance and then immediately taken to hospital, leaving Penny and Steve to make their way back to the office.

Penny wrote up the report on the special incident and Steve phoned the main Field manager in Oventon with the report of what happened in the lobby of the first year dorm. This was not a normal situation. The University was a rather quiet place.

The majority of the students were from the surrounding area of Oventon and Springsville. There were around ten small towns, which could be described today as small hamlets. Many of the residents of those small towns had moved right into Oventon. Maybe that was why the city grew bigger and all the little towns grew smaller.

Penny got back up from where she had been writing. She walked over to Steve and put her arms around his shoulders.

"I sure love a guy with muscles," she said.

"You are just saying that, Penny. We have another round to do, and we are very late."

She gave him a quick kiss on the cheek and then put on her jacket, while grabbing her keys for the round.

The round was very uneventful, until they were walking past the janitor's closet and Steve had a great idea. He was acting on impulse so that his conscience could not talk him out of the idea. Steve stopped and pulled Penny into the closet, without any protest. They held one another and kissed, until Steve realized that they had around five minutes to hit the next sensor. There were certain sensors at certain spots with timers on them. If they were late, they could be called into the President's office for a warning.

The two of them ran very hard until they got to the place just in the nick of time, leaving them both breathless as a result. Penny reached up and the sensor scanned her security key stick, and then she collapsed on the floor, puffing very hard.

"Are you okay?" asked Steve, sounding very concerned.

For some reason Steve was not affected as much as his partner, who held her hands up to indicate that she required some assistance to get up from the floor. As Steve pulled her up, she pulled back on his hands, which made him lose his balance, and then falling on top of her, despite his intention not to do so. But before he could pick himself up, they began kissing.

Finally, Steve pulled himself up from the floor, while reminding Penny of the next sensor which was allocated in the next building. His message sent the two of them running off again; however, on this occasion, they decided to make it a race.

This time round, Steve was the winner; he scanned his key stick before Penny arrived, panting.

"Are you trying to kill me?" she said.

"Boy, you sure are out of shape. Are you working out? Janet always worked out after every shift."

He gazed at her admiringly as she attempted to regain her breath. She was pretty like the twins, however, more down to earth. As Penny sat down on a chair, he decided to make his move.

"Would you like to come over to my place after work?" he asked.

"Sure," she said, "I'd love to hang out with you; however I don't have a babysitter."

"We could hang out at your place if you would like?"

"I'd really like that," she replied, as she got up from the chair to continue with the round.

The rest of the shift went over quickly. There were eight rounds in every shift and the company expected one round every hour. Before they knew it, the two of them were back in the office getting ready to go home.

Steve began putting on his coat while holding his gaze through the mirror at his partner's reflection as she took off her shirt, exposing her red bra. Even though he had just given her a hard time for being out of condition, he admired the shape of her body, and as such, acknowledged that he himself could look better.

They remained silent until they were outside of the first year dorm, when finally, it was Penny who broke the silence. "Have you stopped drooling?" she asked.

"What do you mean, stop drooling?" Steve growled.

"I caught you, young man." She giggled at him, as she grabbed onto his hand.

This was not the only time she had teased him, and what's more, she seemed to enjoy it. Attention like this made Steve feel important. Having been a loner for most of his life, too often had he experienced people making fun of his ways. He was not the average kind of guy, which made him stand out more than others in town.

As they were walking up the main sidewalk, she had pulled his head down toward her and then kissed him on the lips. In the distance he could hear two kids yelling that mommy was coming.

The babysitter was Penny's mother, Tilly, a little, plump old lady who smiled at him when he entered the apartment.

"Good morning, Steve," she said, greeting him with a huge smile.

Steve had known her for as long as he could remember. She had been his grade five, Sunday school teacher in church. So, there was a lot of trust and respect between them, which made it easy for him to have a relationship with her daughter. Tilly really wanted her daughter to find another man who would not cheat on her in the same way that her ex-husband had done. She was almost blind and therefore little did she know that they had been kissing outside of the apartment. Penny thanked her mother for another round of babysitting and kissed her before she set off home.

After her mother had left, she closed the main door and turned her attention to her two kids. Since her mother had fed them breakfast, Penny went to get them dressed for school. Steve helped out by putting on their coats and hats, and given that the local school was just down the street from their apartment, she watched them walk down the street hand in hand. It was rather amusing that her apartment was right across the hall from the Jackson girls and their cousin, Pam, who was also a cousin and had children.

Penny turned round and made her way into the kitchen, and began to wash the dishes that had been gathered from the breakfast table. Steve picked up a towel and started to dry, however, Penny decided to take off her shirt and black security pants, to reveal her red bra and red panties, causing Steve to almost drop one of the plates. She then grabbed a yellow, summer dress from behind the kitchen door and then slipped it on, the dress displaying her curvaceous figure.

"Did you enjoy the show?" she asked Steve, who had returned to dry the dishes.

"What show are you talking about?"

Penny laughed out aloud and walked over to where he was standing. She brushed against him in pretence that there was little room for the two of them, but Steve was fully aware that she had done that on purpose.

"Maybe we should get married before we do something our church would really disapprove of?" she asked, while looking into his face for any sort of a response.

"Do you think that I'm good enough to be a father to your kids?" he asked as he looked out of the kitchen window.

"You will be better than my ex-husband," she said.

"What happened to your ex-husband?"

"He's still in Oventon. I'm not sure who he's going out with. I was told that he'd had a fling with one of the Pastor's daughters in Oventon. They were supposed to get married. The last I've heard was the two of them were made to confess in front of the church. The church ladies had gossiped so much about them, although I believe that they are still living together."

"I thought the church was like a hospital; a place of healing and restoration?"

"Well, I have not had that experience. I always had the impression that only perfect people who do no wrong can belong to the church. The ladies who I know seem to act like their shit does not stink."

"I have read the Bible many times. I never got that impression from Jesus," Steve replied as he picked up a cup of coffee.

"Oh well. I guess that is not what they are reading," she said. "I never heard them talk about Jesus. They seem to talk about the sins of other people who they know in the community. Their talk is always of 'Have you heard the latest' or 'Have you heard about the Pastor's wife sleeping with the choir director?' The last one is not true, of course."

Steve was taken back at how bitter she was against the church of Springsville and of Oventon. There were many other churches that were located in other hamlets, which were scattered around the area. Penny was born in Tillyland, which was on the edge of the huge area surrounding the city of Oventon. She walked over and placed her arms around him and then started to kiss him.

"We have six hours to ourselves before the kids come back from school," she said.

Penny led Steve into the living room and then pinned him down on the couch.

"I was thinking, maybe we should wait until we are married before we have sex," he said.

"Are you tempted to have sex with me?" she asked him and winked.

"I sort of thought it was going in that direction," he replied as he gently pushed her off him.

"What should I be doing?" she asked him, as she walked over to the closet and put her coat on.

Steve could smell the sweet aroma of her perfume, and he looked at her, admiring her figure once again. Unable to resist himself, he made his way over to her and began to kiss her again, sucking on her neck.

"Maybe we should go for a walk to cool down?" she said.

He realized that he may have gone too far, as they were on the verge of making love. Such an act may not disappoint God, Steve thought, but would certainly cause anger among their families. But he had been tempted nevertheless.

They stumbled out the apartment and could feel the neighbors eyes pressed against them as they made their way down the sidewalk. Steve glanced over at Penny's neck, relieved that the mark he'd put on her neck was not visible to the eye.

"I'm sorry that I lost control of myself," he managed to say.

"I'm not complaining," she said.

The two of them went into town and to the restaurant. Many of the church ladies came here to dine, yet mainly to gossip about the locals. The pastors ignored their need to gossip on a regular basis, given that their money was so vital for the church.

Mrs. White, who was one of the leaders in the biggest church here in the town had stated, "We can build a church and we can destroy a church. If the pastors do what they are told, we will build them up. However, go against us and find out how we roll." She laughed as she began her next piece of gossip about the next pastor who dared to talk about the sins which she loved doing. She had decided to spread the word that he was sleeping with his daughter. One week later, another pastor was sent away in dishonor. God doesn't want these things in his church.

As the two of them sat down in the restaurant, they were very careful not to bring attention to themselves. Instead, they ordered burgers and coke and then Steve decided to ask her something that had clearly been on his mind.

"Who was your ex-husband?"

"He was Mrs. White's son."

Steve was shocked at her answer. He could only just stare in disbelief.

"Her son is still the youth pastor of their church!" said Steve.

"Do you think that Mrs. White will tell the honest truth about her son? According to her, her son's shit doesn't stink. She told everybody that I was sleeping around with other men. I was made out to be the bad mother."

"However, the courts gave you the custody of the kids."

"My father has an excellent lawyer. He also promised to reveal their little dirty secret to the entire community."

"What was that secret?" Steve asked curiously.

Penny hushed him by putting her fingers to her lips, and whispered in his ear: "The secret is that her other son had an affair with me. I also get one thousand dollars from the church in order for me to keep quiet and not to have anything to do with my ex-husband or his family."

"But not all the churches are like that one," Steve replied.

As Steve continued to eat his meal he looked over at Penny and observed how similar she was to Janet. He was missing her and began to wonder what she was up to . . . he could hear her voice grow in the distance.

CHAPTER TEN

"OKAY! I WILL ONLY PAY THIS UNTIL THE CHILD IS OF AGE!"

The doctor stood in front of Janet, waiting for her to respond. She stood, unable to move, her mouth wide open in shock. How could she be pregnant?

"I'm shocked at your response," said the doctor. "This is usually a happy time for a husband and wife to find out that they are going to have a first child."

How could she tell this religious man that the man who she had slept with was a married man? Not only was he a married man but he also was one of his co-workers. This was a trusted man who was supposed to help her stop doing drugs. Not only did he help her stop doing drugs, he had helped her become a mother. Fear gripped her soul as she remembered that his wife promised to rearrange her face if she continued seeing her husband.

She left the doctor's office in a complete daze. What should she do? Boy, she really did wish that David was the father of her child. At least they would get married and have a child to raise together. She walked back to her apartment and prepared herself to make the dreaded phone call to Gary. This was not a good day in her short life of twenty years.

Gary was stunned. He told her that she had to have an abortion. This was all against what her mother had taught her. He was rather angry that she did not want to get rid of the problem.

"Are you trying to destroy my marriage?" he yelled.

"You told me that you were separated!" she yelled back at him.

"You really believed that I was telling you the truth?"

"Yes, I thought that since you went to church that you were always a truthful person. You only wanted to get into my pants!" she yelled back even louder.

"You opened your pants up quite nicely and let me right in!" he exclaimed.

"I don't know what to do?" she said, and started to cry.

"Now, please don't cry. There has to be a solution. I will let my lawyer handle this. In order for you to keep quiet and to have money to look after your baby, I will give you one thousand dollars a month."

"Two thousand dollars," she insisted.

"What you little dirty . . ."

"Either you meet my demands or I will go to your pastor's wife and tell her everything," she interrupted.

"Okay! I will only pay this until the child is of age!"

"Deal," she agreed.

After the phone call, Janet sat down and thought things over. And then the phone rang. Some friends were going out that night and therefore invited her to come along. Janet agreed; after all, she needed to have something to get this bad news off her mind.

The evening was eventful. She was careful not to drink alcohol since she was with child. The group went out to a bush party where they had a lot of fun eating hot dogs and most of the kids were drinking.

By the end of the evening they were the last of the cars to leave the lakeside. The driver was stoned, but no one, including Janet, were concerned as they were to busy living in the moment.

The car began racing down a secondary road. Most of the kids had seat belts on, however, since the car was overloaded with passengers, Janet was unable to find one to lock herself in safely. The noise coming from inside the vehicle was excitable, so much so, that they failed to hear the tires screaming as the car swerved out of control. And then everything went dark.

When Janet finally came round she was in an ambulance. She tried to move but she could not. All she could hear were voices around her talking about how she was not responsive, and the screaming of the siren as the ambulance made its way toward its destination. Janet blanked out and once again everything went dark..

Janet was in and out of consciousness and yet still unaware of her surroundings. She tried to speak and move, but was unable to respond.

Janet woke up to find herself sitting in the sand box, which was located in the school's playground. She found herself in the body of a six-year old. David was sitting there with her in the sand box. They played together as her sister Shannon had gone into the bathroom. Then suddenly a bee stung her. David put some cool mud on her and it made her feel so much better. She felt at peace in her soul.

Then she found herself in the University's security office. She was kissing David, but this time in an adult's body. As they made out, she could feel his eyes watching her. She felt his presence as she walked with him on the many rounds that they did do together.

Janet woke up and opened her eyes to the sight of her loved ones sitting around the hospital bed. They appeared to be oblivious to the fact that she had regained consciousness and continued to ignore her as they talked to one another. They were acting as if she was in a coma, or so she thought. And then she drifted out of consciousness until the early hours of the morning when she awoke and called out for a nurse. When the nurse answered her call, Janet asked if David was around.

The nurse let her know that he had left six hours ago, but would let Janet know if she saw him again. It was four days later when she was made aware that Shannon and David had been in to see her. She didn't want her sister to know that she was awake, not yet, so played dumb when both of them visited her. Janet's mother was also unaware that she had regained consciousness, however, when Mrs. Jackson finally left the hospital, Janet made her sister aware that she had pulled through. Shannon squealed with delight. Janet asked her sister if she could speak with David alone.

David listened intently as Janet discussed the special parts of their relationship. She didn't give him any reason to believe that she knew what was going on between him and her sister, which surprised David, so much so, that he gazed at her with an open mouth.

When he left the room, Shannon returned to her sister's bedside. Janet told her that she had ended her relationship with David because he wanted more than she was able to offer. As for the switch that they had played so often on the past –their secret was safe, leaving Shannon smiling as she left the room.

Chapter Eleven

"It was while they were rounding the corner of the apartment when he noticed David slamming the door to the Jackson's car."

It was the next morning when Steve awoke to the phone ringing. He noticed that the phone call was coming from Shannon, Janet's twin sister. When he answered the phone, Shannon was quite upset about something.

"Shannon, please slow down. I didn't understand one word that you've just jabbered."

"Janet was in a car accident last night," Shannon sobbed out.

"What happened?" Steve asked.

Shannon told him that somehow the car that Janet had been traveling in had hit a train that was at the crossing five miles out of Oventon. Janet was the only survivor from the car crash, and her life was hanging by the skin of her teeth. Shannon told him that she had gone to visit her the night before with David, and they were planning on going to visit her again soon.

Penny and Steve had gone home after they had left the restaurant. They had to get home just before three o'clock as that was when the kids would arrive home from school. Steve had spent time with her helping her with the kids. He even got to help bath the two youngsters then put them right into their beds.

When the kids had gone to bed, Penny and Steve relaxed on the couch together. Penny was now dressed in her pajamas; old-fashioned top and bottoms, which were red with pink hearts. Steve approved and, more so, when she started to cuddle and kiss him. He thought she was a great kisser, which made the experience all the more enjoyable.

The phone call had changed everything for Steve. He was supposed to meet up with Penny at her place; however, when he eventually arrived, Penny was already preparing the kids for school. Today of all days, Steve and Penny had the day off from the University, which meant that it was a perfect time for him to go and see Janet.

As she fed the kids breakfast, he explained what Shannon had told him about her sister's accident. Penny was shocked; this was not the kind of everyday thing that you heard about, especially in Springsville.

Penny was able to borrow her mother's car. The two of them drove out of the small town and onto the highway that led to the big city of Oventon. Steve had never been away from Springsville in his entire life. This was the first time that he had drove in a car outside of the town. So this was a brand new experience for him.

Penny drove while Steve gazed from the window at the farmers who were out working on their fields. Penny glanced over to him and asked if he was okay. He nodded and was appreciative of her driving ability.

In the huge city hospital, the two of them walked in silence. Steve knew that she was just as worried as he was about their friend, Janet. He had read in many story books all about accidents and how many times the people who were in the intensive care would die in the end.

They walked into the intensive care unit and saw David and Shannon standing by the window, looking into the room at Janet. They were shocked to see her in such a dreadful condition.

Steve was not sure what to say to David, since he had known what had gone on during their relationship together. He acknowledged what a huge let down that must have been for him.

Since there was little more that either of them could do, they all decided to go and get something to eat at the pizza place around the corner from the hospital. While they sat at the table eating, Steve was certain that he'd heard Shannon say that she was pregnant and about to get married.

It was later when Steve and Penny went back to the car and began the drive home. Penny remained quiet while she drove. When it came to life or death situations, she had great difficulty coping with the idea. She remained deep in thought for the remainder of the journey back to Springsville.

When they came round the corner to the apartment, Steve noticed David slamming the door of the Jackson's car. He saw Shannon walking after him calling him back as he stormed down towards his place. David sure looked very upset and disturbed.

Penny stopped the car and walked over to Shannon. Steve could not hear the conversation that was taking place between them, only the two of them hugging before Penny gave her a kiss on the cheek. Steve had heard some time ago that such an act meant that they were gay, a saying that he strongly dismissed, knowing that such behavior was common amongst women.

Steve had heard that David had told people at the nursing home that Nancy Grace was gay. He had found that hard to believe. Nancy Grace was not a very nice person. She made the old men drool and the old women cry. She sure loved the old men.

Penny eventually got back into the car and the two of them drove in silence. She pulled up outside of her mother's house, and by the time they got to the front door, the kids were ready to leave. Penny told her mother about their unexpected trip that day. After bidding her mother farewell, they headed back to the apartment in deep discussion, when Steve asked her something that was at the forefront of his mind: "What were you and Shannon talking about?" he asked curiously.

She looked a little embarrassed and giggled. "It was only girl's stuff. You wouldn't understand."

Steve began to make supper when they returned to the apartment. It was his idea to have vegetable soup with tuna buns. He was always fond of making homemade soup and the kids really enjoyed it, finishing everything he put before them, much to the satisfaction of their mother.

The kids yelled goodnight from their bedrooms and then Steve sat down on the couch next to Penny. She looked hot; her hair was tied up in a bun and she smiled with approval as he put his arm around her. The mark on her neck was now visible, which made him feel good. She was his woman—and he wanted the whole town to know it.

"Which movie would you like to watch, sweetheart?" she asked.

Her question really shocked the daylights out of him. This was the first time she had used the word sweetheart. She seemed to becoming more relaxed about being around him.

After some discussion, the two of them had decided to watch the movie, *The young Riders*. It was a good country and western show, which both of them really enjoyed.

As they were watching the movie, Steve leaned over and snuggled right close to her. He really enjoyed such times that made their relationship worthwhile. Her perfume smelled like roses. She really seemed to enjoy his company. They started to kiss passionately, and from that moment, were forgetful of the movie.

Chapter Twelve

"You are alive!" she exclaimed.

As the days went by, Janet felt a lot better. Her doctor, Larry Cooter, always came by her room at least twice a day. The tubes had been removed from her body and she was now in the main part of the hospital. Shannon, David and her mother came to visit quite often. In the hospital, she had a lot of time to think about her future and the direction her life was headed in.

She knew deep inside that she had had a brush with death. This in itself really gave her a new perspective on life. She had spent many hours reading her Bible and other books, which Shannon had borrowed from the church's library. Janet remembered that she was pregnant, and furthermore, what she would now do.

It really bothered her that her doctor felt that she should stay for another three days. She wanted to get back to the University so she could get her life back to normal.

As she sat there in her room, she started to think ahead. Gary was not willing to leave his wife and he was paying her two thousand dollars a month in order to keep quiet about the entire affair. She wanted her baby to have a father figure. If the baby was a boy, she would name the baby Robert, and if the baby was a girl, she would name the baby Rose. *Now,* she wondered, *it was just a case of who would take up the role of the father?*

David had walked by Janet's room; he was lost and was trying to find her. And that was when it came to her, the solution to all her problems: David would be the father. After his visit she started to write down the lines that she would say to him when the time came to ask for his hand in marriage.

It was around two days later when her doctor, Larry, had walked into her room. She smiled at him as he sat down at the foot of her bed. "So, how is the mother doing?" he asked with a very friendly smile.

"I am doing fine. Can I go home today, Doctor?" she asked impatiently.

"You certainly can," he said.

"I will get my things together and I can be ready right away."

"Now, calm down, mother. You don't need to hurry."

It was a huge relief when she was dropped off at the apartment where the girls were staying. She could hardly wait to see her cousin and friend Penny. She was made well aware that Penny had been seeing her work partner Steve on the side. Shannon had filled her in to what the gossip was going around about those two. She had heard that the two of them had been sleeping together. However, the gossip didn't end there; the word on the street was that David was sleeping with Shannon and they had a child together.

She wanted to hear from her directly what was going on. As she unpacked her bags, she really felt so grateful to be home. That did not change the fact that she was still pregnant. In order for her plan to work, she had to move fast on putting that plan into motion. However, she had one matter to deal with first, so she walked across the hall and knocked on the door.

Penny answered the door, with a look of surprise on her face. She threw her arms around her cousin and gave her a huge hug.

"You are alive!" she exclaimed.

"I sure am. I had a lot of time to do some soul searching. This accident really opened my eyes to what the priorities are in my life."

"I'm only happy that you're alive. You could have been killed!"

"I know. I was the only person out of seven who walked away from that crash."

The two of them walked into the living room and sat down.

"So," said Janet, "how are you and Steve doing?"

"Good. I believe that I've found the right one for me."

"Have you guys made love yet?"

"That's a very personal question, Janet."

Penny looked very shocked and hurt by what Janet had just asked. Janet knew that she was prying into her personal life, but that did little to prevent her asking the question, and from that point, she continued to explain what it was that she had planned to do over the coming days.

"I believe that I'm in love with David," said Janet.

"What!" Penny exclaimed in a state of shock.

"The accident has really put things in perspective. Before the accident, I was carefree and made a lot of bad decisions; now, it's opened my eyes and I realize that life is too short. I don't want to make any more bad choices with my life."

"I heard that you and Gary were sleeping together," said Penny.

"Well, that relationship sort of went south or to hell in a hand basket," she replied, with her head hanging down.

"What happened?" asked Penny.

"He's married."

"Janet! What on earth were you thinking of sleeping with a married man?"

"Penny! That was rather rude."

"Well you were rather rude when you asked me if I slept with Steve. Janet, my relationship with Steve is none of your business."

"My relationship with Dr. Gary is none of yours!" Janet snapped back in a huge fit of anger, and with that, Janet got up and left the apartment, slamming the door behind her. Penny's reaction had made her angry. There was much more that she wanted to say to Penny, however, as she was muttering her threats, she heard a voice behind her.

"Would a bowl of pickles and ice-cream help?"

Janet swung round to give the person a piece of her mind, but to her shock, she was confronted by her mother, who was standing there with her hands on her hips. Janet could contain herself no longer and fell into her mother's arms and sobbed uncontrollably, leaving her mother to comfort her.

"Now, maybe you better go over there and mend your relationship with Penny. You're going to need all the friends that you can have on your side."

Janet knew better than to argue with her mother, so she walked across the hallway to see her neighbor, and as she did so, she couldn't help but wonder how Steve was doing. She sure hoped that Penny was treating him well. It dawned on her that those two were just perfect for each other. She just hoped that she did not make a mess of their relationship.

CHAPTER THIRTEEN

"ARE YOU SLEEPING WITH HER?"

After spending time with Penny, Steve arrived at work and went straight into the office to look at the schedule. Now that Janet was back to working full time, Penny was reduced to part time, covering days off and weekend working. Steve missed her already; having become accustomed to Janet's bad work habits, he hoped that her time in Oventon had mended her ways.

Steve was surprised to see Janet as she walked in ten minutes early, she was well dressed and more presentable in her apprearance.

As they went on their first round, Steve was shocked that Janet no longer had her hands on him like she did before. She was very well behaved, so much so that when he asked her what was going in her life right now, she responded by giggling and then told him that she had turned over a new leaf. They continued on their round, and having hit all the first round sensors five minutes early than would be expected of them, they were looking good for bonus points, which they would achieve if all twenty sensors were hit five to six minutes early.

The dining room was their final stop, so they made themselves a cup of coffee along with some cookies that Janet had baked. "So," said Janet, "When did you and Penny start dating?"

"So, when did you leave to go to Oventon?" he responded, deliberately disregarding her question.

Janet smiled and sipped her coffee. She realized that right now she had no dirt on him. Steve was unaware that she was pregnant, which suited her just fine. He'd ignored her last question regarding his relationship with Penny, so she decided to try again. "Are you sleeping with her?" she asked.

"No!" said Steve.

"How can you have the self control in order to stop you from jumping her bones?"

"I'm telling you the truth. We have not gone all of the way."

"I think that you're lying."

"I'm telling you the truth. I want to save my body for when we decide to get married."

"Marriage! Marriage is only a piece of paper created by the church so they can make money," she said.

Steve was shocked to hear her talk this way. His views on marriage were very sacred.

"Did Adam and Eve get married by a preacher in a church?" she asked.

"No," said Steve, "God married them. Jesus and Paul talked about marriage as being important."

"However, I don't believe there was any mention of living in sin?"

Steve was in no mood to argue. There was no use arguing, especially with a female Jackson. There was no way he could win, so instead, he made them both another cup of coffee.

Janet sipped her coffee and gazed at Steve with an expression of innocence. With nothing more to say, she got up and left the room, Steve following her as they made their way back to the office.

Steve started the eleven to six shift the following day. There would be two different shifts being worked this day, Penny and Janet would be working together later that night. When he arrived at work, he was surprised to see Janet sitting in the office.

"I am working on the schedule. Could you please leave me alone for about one hour?" she asked.

"Sure. I will do my first round. Call me on the radio if you need me," he said.

As Steve walked out into the lobby, he noticed David making his way into the building. He appeared to be somewhat nervous, which made Steve wonder what was going on. Janet had been acting strange that morning too. Her secrecy had made him curious; however, she was looking quite healthy and he was happy that she was now free of drugs and alcohol. Most of all, he considered that she was looking happy.

Steve was walking into one of the classrooms when his phone rang. At a glance, he could see that the call was coming from the security office, so he answered in a professional manner: "Jackson University, Steve speaking. How may I help you?"

"We're engaged!" Janet's excited, out of control voice came over the cell phone.

Steve was speechless. For a brief moment there was confusion in his mind, and then it suddenly came to him. Janet had asked David to marry him, and he had accepted her proposal. It now made sense to him why Janet had been backing away from him lately. She had decided to get back with her ex-boyfriend.

For Steve, the pieces of his life were finally coming together.

CHAPTER FOURTEEN

"IT WAS DURING THE DANCE WHILE HE WAS DANCING WITH HER."

No sooner had Steve finished talking to Janet, he then immediately called Penny to inform her of the news. He was surprised to learn however, that Penny had known of Janet's intentions all along.

"I've heard that she's pregnant," said Penny. "Do you think she is with child?"

"She doesn't look like she is. She seemed to be very pleasant here at work."

"I've noticed that she's been moody ever since she came back from the big city," said Penny. "These are signs of someone who has filled their pants."

"Filled their pants?" Steve questioned. "She did not actually shit herself."

"Oh silly, it is a term that means that someone is pregnant." Penny giggled.

Steve and Penny remained undecided whether Janet was indeed pregnant; however, it was a week later when they both attended David and Janet's wedding, when the subject came up again.

"I really do believe that she is putting on weight," Penny remarked.

"I really believe that you have a great imagination," said Steve.

The discussion was closed for now. The wedding was delightful in many ways, the food was much to Steve's liking, however, their taste in music perhaps lacking, or so he thought. He was proud to be sitting there with Penny and her two daughters, with a warm feeling that they were a family.

Penny studied Janet and questioned how someone so attractive could be with a man who was not as good looking. Steve ate his meal while admiring the woman who eventually would be his future wife. Penny was wearing a pink dress with a very low neck line, which made her look wonderful. Steve was aware that the local gossipers were present in the room, and as such, acknowledged that they were taking note, making an assumption no doubt that he and Penny and the children, were living in sin.

It was later while Steve and Penny got up to dance that she dropped to her knees and asked him for his hand in marriage. He immediately said yes, and then kissed her. As they made their way back from the dance floor, a lady from Mrs. White's group called out: "Why did you not get married before having children? You two have been living in sin!"

Mrs.White responded to her comments loud and clear: "Mary Beth," she said, "why don't you just shut your huge trap! This is none of your business."

It's so funny when there are things to hide. The web which we weave makes God unhappy. It is too bad that we just can't be honest.

Steve and Penny danced, while fully aware that they were hiding the affair of Mrs. White's son; David and Janet danced, Janet holding the secret of her pregnancy, and more so, the father of her child, none of them willing to expose the secrets that they held.

Penny was delighted that Steve had accepted her proposal of marriage. Their situation was a little out of the ordinary; most couples that they were aware of got married before having children. She was going to get married again but under different circumstances, those of which were simply out of her control.

Penny sat down with Steve and asked him: "Are we hiding anything from each other, or from God for that matter?"

Their lives had been affected by Janet's experience, webs that they had allowed to be weaved would no doubt influence the remainder of their lives.

Steve thought for a moment as he considered the question she had asked him: "We have to examine our lives, Penny," he said. "We must be honest wth each other and expose the webs which we have built into our lives. We are not responsible for other people's actions or for those who clearly don't know any better."

Steve looked at Penny and smiled. He knew deep in his heart that he had now found the right person, and while walking home that night, he was overwhelmed by a feeling of deep peace within him. He reflected on his experience with Janet and then with Penny. Janet was now back with David and they were now on their honeymoon together. Life had fallen into place. It appeared to him that we as humans mess things up, leaving God to repair any damage.

Steve looked up into the night sky and saw a shooting star pass by. He made a wish before continuing on his way home. When he finally returned to the apartment the phone was ringing, and upon answering it, he was met by the voice of his sweetheart.

"I'm thinking of you," she said.

"I really miss you already," he said. "I can't wait to get married to you."

"I feel the same way."

They ended the call after hours of chatting. Steve realized that the web that they had weaved was now slowly coming together into something far greater than he could have previously imagined. As he lay in bed, he looked out of his window and watched as another shooting star passed by. *The webs we weave*, he thought. *God makes good of our choices and makes them into something more beautiful than we could ever possibly imagine.*

ABOUT THE BOOK

It is the web which we weave when we first begin to deceive.
Everybody has cobwebs in dark closets in their lives. This sequel
to "The RSA adventure – The untold story now revealed" now goes
back in time to the events which David wrote about in his journal
when he became a resident in the same nursing home where he
had worked for the past thirty-five years. This time the events
were written in time from the point of view of Janet and Steve
who were security guards at the town's University. For every story
there is always another side of that story. These events were like
an exciting roller coaster ride loaded with tons of surprises and of
course this ride ends in a way which no one could ever predict. I
dare you to come along for the ride of your life. Revisit the events
of the first book and experience them in a different way. Yes, the
web which we weave when we first start to deceive.

ABOUT THE AUTHORS

Lorne W.P Vanderwoude lives with his wife in Camrose, Alberta. Leslie Liddle lives with her husband in Bawlf, Alberta. It was while the two of them were at work when they discovered how much they loved to write. Leslie was one of the editors of the "The RSA Adventure – The untold story now revealed." The two of them got together to help create this newest book, now written as a sequel to this first novel.

There were a few problems that came up when the first book was released. There were a few errors which had slipped through the editors as well as the author. In order to correct this, more editors were hired to ensure that the novel would be as perfect as possible. The second problem (which was revealed to us by our readers), was that the flashbacks were sometimes confusing. These were scaled back and used very seldom to help clear up the confusion.

Lorne and Leslie really enjoy creating stories. This newest book is yet another dream of Lorne's. He had always wanted to co-author a book with another author who also shares his love for telling stories. Lorne always had believed the saying that, "Two heads are better than one." Now this is another dream that Lorne is now fulfilling. His dream of writing a book with a second author.

CPSIA information can be obtained at www.ICGtesting.com
Printed in the USA
LVOW09s1911191214

419661LV00009B/91/P